A Gift For:

_____

From:

_____

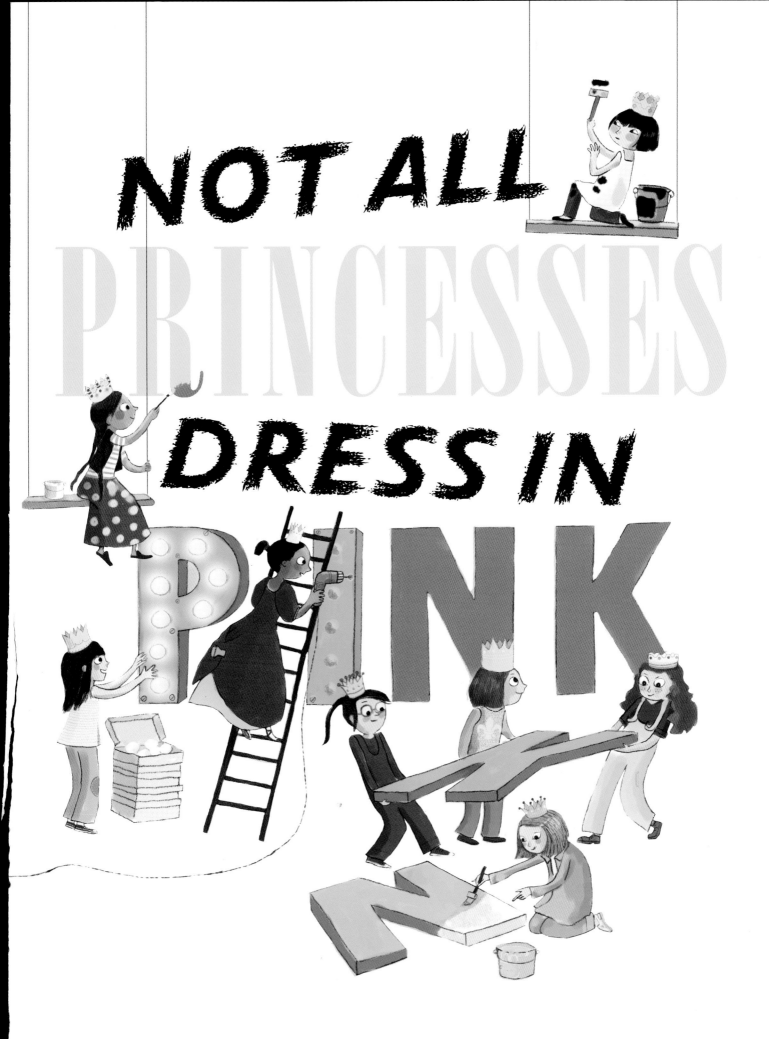

For my special Stemple princesses,
Caroline Lee and Amelia Hyatt.
And a shout-out to Sophia DiTerlizzi
—J. Y.

To three princesses I adore, Abigail
and Emma Lindwall, and Natalie Aquadro,
some of whom wear pink—H. E. Y. S.

To Elsa and Rosalie, my princesses
who are hiding somewhere in these pages
—A.-S. L.

SIMON & SCHUSTER BOOKS FOR YOUNG READERS
An imprint of Simon & Schuster Children's Publishing Division
1230 Avenue of the Americas, New York, New York 10020
Text copyright © 2010 by Jane Yolen and Heidi E. Y. Stemple
Illustrations copyright © 2010 by Anne-Sophie Lanquetin

This edition published in 2010 by Hallmark Books, a division of Hallmark Cards Inc.,
under license from Simon & Schuster Books for Young Readers,
an Imprint of Simon & Schuster Children's Publishing Division.

Visit us on the Web at www.Hallmark.com.

Book design by Lucy Ruth Cummins
The text for this book is set in Family Cat.
The illustrations for this book are rendered digitally.

ISBN: 978-1-59530-350-9
Printed and bound in China
BOK1165
JAN11

first
edition

Not All Princesses Dress in Pink

By Jane Yolen and Heidi E. Y. Stemple

Illustrated by Anne-Sophie Lanquetin

Simon & Schuster Books for Young Readers
New York   London   Toronto   Sydney

Hallmark
GIFT BOOKS

Not all princesses dress in pink.
Some play in bright red socks that stink,

blue team jerseys that don't quite fit,
accessorized with a baseball mitt,

and a *sparkly crown.*

Some princesses, when they choose,
never pick out fancy shoes,

but soccer cleats for outdoor sports
with shin guards and some baggy shorts,

and a *sparkly crown*.

Some princesses roll around,
wrestling on the muddy ground,

then get right up to skip and dance
in tattered, stained, and muddy pants,

and a *sparkly crown.*

Some princesses wear their jewels
while fixing things with power tools:
saw, screwdriver, hammer, drill,

they wear with pride each greasy spill

and a *sparkly crown.*

Some princesses break their nails
planting flowers into pails,
driving dump trucks, moving dirt,
dressed in an extra-large hand-me-down shirt,

and a *sparkly crown.*

Some princesses like to pedal
wearing lots of shiny metal:
helmet on head, and body armor,
so that nothing bad can harm her

or her *sparkly crown*.

In chain mail they easily fight
an evil sorcerer or knight,

or escape a stony tower,
displaying all their princess power

in a *sparkly crown*.

Then after a great victory lap
(followed by a well-earned nap),
to the ball these princesses run,
wearing no pink gowns—not one!

They waltz in red, fox-trot in blue,
they reel in plaid and polka dots, too.
And in those grand and fancy halls,
one even hip-hops in her overalls —

and a *very sparkly princess crown.*

If you have enjoyed this book
or it has touched your life
in some way, we would love
to hear from you.

Please send your comments to:
Hallmark Book Feedback
P.O. Box 419034
Mail Drop 215
Kansas City, MO 64141

Or e-mail us at:
booknotes@hallmark.com